Arthur and the Goalie Ghost

A Marc Brown **GOOD SPORTS** Chapter Book

Arthur and the Goalie Ghost

Text by Stephen Krensky

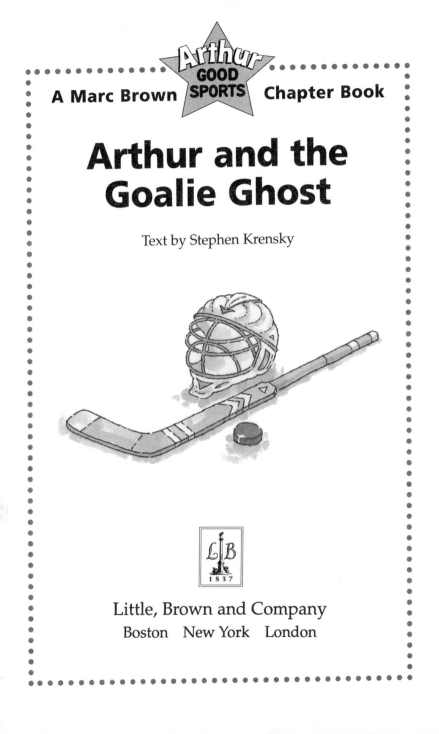

LᛰB
1837

Little, Brown and Company
Boston   New York   London

Text has been reviewed and assigned a reading level by Laurel S. Ernst,
M.A., Teachers College, Columbia University, New York, New York;
reading specialist, Chappaqua, New York.

Library of Congress Cataloging-in-Publication Data

Krensky, Stephen.
    Arthur and the goalie ghost / text by Stephen Krensky. — 1st ed.
    p. cm. — (A Marc Brown Arthur good sports chapter book ; bk. 5)
    Summary: Arthur and his hockey teammates, as well as the ghost of the
greatest goalie of all time, help out when Buster worries he'll never be as
good a goalie as his hero.
    ISBN 0-316-07304-0
    [1. Hockey — Fiction. 2. Self-confidence — Fiction. 3. Ghosts — Fiction
4. Animals — Fiction.] I. Title.
PZ7.K883 Aqf2001
[Fic] — dc21   2001029440

10 9 8 7 6 5 4 3 2

LAKE (hc)
COM-MO (pb)

Printed in the United States of America

For Miles Criffield

Chapter 1

• • • • • • • • • • •

"Goalie?" said Arthur. "You want to be a goalie?"

Buster nodded. They were walking home from school on a windy fall day. Hockey season was starting, and the first practice was coming up.

"It's where the action is," said Buster. "The last line of defense. Besides, I was reading this new biography about Jacques Nettoyer, the greatest goalie of all time. He's my favorite hockey player."

"I know," said Arthur. "You've only told me five million times."

Buster smiled. "And now it's five million and one. It was a sad day for hockey when Jacques passed away. Did you know that every team in the league sent a representative to his funeral? It's the only time that's ever happened. And they raised a great arch of hockey sticks for him at the end of the service."

"You have mentioned it a few —"

"Well, in this book, Jacques was asked to name the three best positions in hockey. And do you know what he said? His choices were one: goalie, two: goalie, and three: goalie."

"What a surprise," said Arthur.

"I know, I know, but he was very convincing when he talked about it. And remember that Greek myth about Atlas holding the world on his shoulders? Well, Jacques says that's what a goalie does for his team."

Arthur nodded. "So does that mean you're going to need broad shoulders?"

Buster flexed his muscles. "I'm working on it already."

"Well, I'm impressed," said Arthur. "I don't think I'd want to be a goalie. All those pucks whizzing around."

"You have to be fast," said Buster, bobbing his head back and forth. "And nimble."

"And then there's the pressure," Arthur went on.

Buster stopped in his tracks. "Pressure? What pressure?"

"You know, when the wing fakes out the defense and comes in to score. That isn't the goalie's fault, but nobody ever blames the defense."

"They don't?"

Arthur shook his head. "Nope. They always blame the goalie, because when the

3

puck gets by him, that's the last thing they see."

Buster looked uncomfortable for a moment. "I hadn't thought about that."

Suddenly, Buster blinked. He thought he saw the ghost of Jacques Nettoyer, on Arthur's right, standing in full uniform.

"Do not be alarmed," said the ghost. *"I have come to help you."*

"What are you doing here?" asked Buster.

"Huh?" said Arthur. "Where do you think I've been?"

Buster realized Arthur did not see the ghost. "Um . . . oh, nowhere. I was just thinking of something else. Sorry."

"As I said, I have come to help you," the ghost added. Then he faded away.

"You're just nervous," said Arthur. "That's okay. This is a new league. The crowds won't be very big. So it's not like a lot of people

4

will see you. You won't be under the microscope or anything."

Buster brightened. "You're right," he said, glancing again at where the ghost had been. "I guess I have nothing to worry about."

Chapter 2

• • • • • • • • • • •

Buster's mother, Bitsy Baxter, sat behind her desk at the newspaper office. She was staring at the ceiling and chewing on a pencil. The office was crowded; books and articles covered every surface. But today it felt especially crowded, because Bitsy was having a meeting. Several of her reporters stood around her, ready to take notes.

"We need a new feature," she said. "Every week it's the same thing — bake sales, budget meetings, park dedications. . . . What about something with more human interest? Something closer to home that people here can relate to. Something fresh. Something with heart. Any ideas?"

One reporter had a thought. "How about that guy who wrestles alligators with one hand?"

She frowned. "Isn't that the guy who only has one hand?"

"I guess so. But he used to have two — before the accident, that is."

Mrs. Baxter shook her head. "I don't think our readers want to be learning about missing body parts over their breakfast cereal."

"What about a cat getting stuck in a tree?" asked another reporter. "The fire engine could come. There would be a big rescue. People love reading about stuff like that."

Mrs. Baxter sighed. "I'm sure they do. There's just one little problem. . . . "

"What's that?"

"Do you know of any cats stuck in trees at the moment?"

"Uh, no," the reporter admitted.

"Do you plan to put a cat up a tree any time soon?" asked Mrs. Baxter. "That is, are you going to manufacture the story yourself?"

The reporter slumped against the wall. "I guess not."

"Well, then, I guess we won't be able to rely on the cats to make things interesting for us."

The phone rang.

"Hold on a second," said Mrs. Baxter. She picked up the phone. "Hello? Oh, hi, Buster. . . . No, I haven't forgotten. . . . Yes, yes, I know it's important to be on time. But have I ever been late? Uh-huh. . . . Uh-huh. . . . Okay, Buster, you've made your point. It's a new team, a new league, and you don't want the coach mad at you right from the start. . . . Fine, I'll see you later, then. Bye."

She hung up the phone. "Sorry about

that. Buster's all excited about playing on this new hockey team. Now, where were we?"

"Hunting for a new feature," said the first reporter.

The second reporter was smiling. "You say it's a new team?"

"That's right."

"Maybe we could do a story on that. You know, what it's like to start with a clean slate, to hope for a championship."

Mrs. Baxter nodded. "It has possibilities. Keep going."

"We could follow the team for a few games, charting their ups and downs. We could go deep, really getting under the surface." He paused. "Of course, if you think it would be a problem for Buster, then we shouldn't do it."

Mrs. Baxter laughed. "My Buster? He loves being the center of attention. For him this will be a dream come true."

Chapter 3

• • • • • • • • • • • •

The Elwood City Flyers skated slowly
around the rink at the start of their first
practice. Each player (except the goalies)
had a puck on a stick and was softly bat-
ting it in a zigzag pattern. Coach Simard
was standing in the middle of the ice,
shouting out comments as they passed.

Buster was not part of this procession.
As one of the goalies, he was squatting
and stretching near the goal. He had just
finished roughing up the ice directly in
front of the goalmouth. This would pro-
vide some resistance to his skates when
making sudden movements. Jacques Net-

toyer had written about the importance of this preparation in his book *Goalie for Life*.

"You are ready, yes?"

Buster blinked. It was Jacques Nettoyer again — standing next to him. True, he was a little gray and wispy, but there was no mistaking him. Buster looked around. Nobody else seemed to be paying any attention. Again, Buster was the only one who could see the goalie ghost.

"You have the best job in the whole world," said the ghost. *"The fate of your team rests squarely on your shoulders. You control its fate. You control its destiny. There is nothing better than that!"*

"I guess," Buster muttered.

"You guess what?" Arthur had come up to the goal.

"Oh . . . um . . ." Buster shrugged. "I guess I'm ready for the photographers."

"What photographers?" asked Arthur.

"You haven't heard?"

"Heard what?"

"The newspaper is going to cover our team in depth as we begin our season. It's going to be a big feature," said Buster.

Arthur looked surprised. "Are we going to be interviewed?"

"I think so, but —"

Coach Simard blew his whistle. "All right, Flyers, gather 'round. We're going to start with a shooting drill. Buster will be in goal, and we don't want him shell-shocked so early in the season. So nothing fancy now — no hard slap shots, no flipping the puck. This is just a warm-up. Understand? Good. Then let's get to it."

Buster took up his position in front of the net.

"You must get lower," said Jacques. *"No part of your body should be wasted above the net. Everything should be part of the Great Wall, the Barrier Reef. . . ."*

The skaters stood in two groups at opposite ends of the blue line. Binky was the first skater. He came in from the left, faked once, and then fired — into the upper-right corner.

"*What are you, a statue?*" said Jacques. "*Are you waiting for pigeons to sit on your shoulders?*"

"I'm trying," Buster muttered.

"*You must move when they move, see the shot in their eyes before they take it.*"

The next three skaters all scored as well. Buster fell twice trying to stop them. The next puck he stopped, but only because the Brain accidentally hit him in the stomach.

"This is harder than it looks," said Buster.

Jacques sighed. "*It appears,*" he said, "*that we have much work to do.*"

Chapter 4

• • • • • • • • • • •

The next day at noon, the cafeteria at Lakewood Elementary was filled with hungry students. The cafeteria lady, Mrs. McGrady, was beaming because it was pizza day and she was doing a brisk business.

At one of the tables, Francine was sitting with Muffy, the Brain, Arthur, and Binky.

"I can't believe Mr. Ratburn is creating a penalty box for our homework," said Francine.

"It does sound a little intimidating," said the Brain. "He said he got the idea from a hockey game."

"That just shows you the danger of watching too much sports," said Muffy.

Binky grunted. "Just because your homework has a few spelling mistakes shouldn't mean it should go in a penalty box."

"But it doesn't have to stay there," said Arthur. "Once you correct the mistakes, the homework comes out."

"Well, I still don't like it," said Francine, taking a big bite of pizza.

Binky frowned. "I'll bet Buster doesn't, either," he said. "His homework was the first to be penalized."

"Where is Buster, anyway?" said Muffy.

"There he is!" said Arthur, waving. "Over here, Buster!" he called out.

Buster walked over and nodded to his classmates. *"Bonjour, mes amis,"* he said.

"Bonjour?" said Arthur.

"Oui," said Buster. "That means 'yes.' *Bonjour* means 'hello.' *Mes amis* means 'my friends.' "

"Then why don't you just say, 'Hi, guys'?" asked Binky. "It would be easier."

Buster shook his head. *"Ah, non, Monsieur Binky."*

"Can you explain — in English — why you're speaking French?" asked the Brain.

Buster sighed. "I thought it might help if I spoke like Jacques. It's a strategy. The more Jacques things I do, the more I'll be like Jacques. And since Jacques was such a great goalie, it will help me be a better goalie, too."

He put his lunch box on the table.

"Buster, it's pizza day," said Arthur. "You *brought* your lunch?"

Buster nodded. "Jacques had very particular ideas about food." He took out a sandwich.

Binky took a sniff. "What's that?" he asked, making a face.

"Peanut butter and tuna fish."

"Mixed together?" said Francine.

"Vomitrocious!" said Muffy.

"Let me guess," said the Brain. "One of Jacques's favorites?"

"*Oui,*" said Buster.

"But you hate tuna fish," said Arthur.

"That's not important. What matters is that Jacques liked it. He wrote that tuna was brain food and that eating it with peanut butter made it stick with him better."

"You're taking this Jacques stuff a little too far, aren't you?" asked Arthur.

"*Mais non,*" said Buster. "I must do whatever it takes. The team is counting on me. The fans are counting on me. And I'm sure Jacques is counting on me, too."

"That's a lot of responsibility," Arthur pointed out.

"*C'est vrai,*" said Buster, forcing down the first bite of his sandwich. "That is the truth."

Chapter 5

• • • • • • • • • • • • •

Buster sat on the bench lacing up his skates. He carefully double-knotted the loops to keep them from coming undone.

"Not too tight," Jacques said. "You do not wish to cut off the circulation and put your feet to sleep. But not too loose, either, or you will stumble around like a baby learning to walk."

Buster nodded and finished up. This first game was against the Seals, and he had heard they were pretty good.

"Hey, Buster!"

It was Jimmy Jolsen, one of the reporters from the newspaper.

"Hi, Jimmy," said Buster.

"Do you mind if I ask you a few questions? You don't need to put on your game face or anything, do you?"

"Be polite to the members of the press," said Jacques, *"so that they will properly note your achievements."*

"No, no, I'm all set. Fire away."

"That's a good one — coming from a goalie." Jimmy took out his pen and pad. "What's it like being the last line of defense?" he asked. "What goes through your mind in those final seconds before you have to react?"

"You must move like lightning," said Jacques. *"You must be a blur, a flash. . . ."*

"I have to move like lightning," said Buster.

"Faster than a speeding bullet, perhaps?" said Jimmy, smiling.

"No!" said Jacques. *"The speeding bullet is too slow. It is a worm, a turtle. In the net, you must be as fast as thought itself."*

Buster couldn't remember all that. "I do the best I can," he said, smiling.

When the game started, the players skated cautiously at first, getting a sense of one another's moves. But finally a Seal forward dumped the puck into the Flyers' zone, and the wings flew after it.

Buster lined himself up with the goalpost, but even so, he was caught off-guard as the puck ricocheted off someone's skate and shot across the middle.

Buster rushed to the other goalpost, but he could feel nervousness creeping up on him. So many things were happening at once. It was different from practice. Buster could almost feel the energy from the other players around him. And then, a sudden shift and a Seal fired a shot.

GOAL!

The puck had slipped right through Buster's legs.

"A rookie mistake," said Jacques. *"Learn from it. You must bend your knees toward each other so that there is no room for a puck to get by."*

Buster tried, but the action moved so quickly. . . . Before the end of the first period, the Seals scored again.

Jacques was not pleased. *"Think like a cat, not an elephant! Why is that so hard for you to remember?"*

Buster didn't know. He was trying to play exactly like Jacques. He had pictured himself lunging and leaping, kicking and diving. He had memorized every word Jacques had written about the way he moved. But reading about it and doing it were not the same thing.

When the game ended, the Flyers had lost, 6–2. Buster felt terrible. As he moved down the line of Seal players, shaking hands, he could feel the disappointment of the home crowd.

And out of the corner of his eye, Buster could see Jimmy Jolsen scribbling furiously on his pad. Buster could not see what he was writing, but whatever it was, Buster was sure he wasn't going to like it.

Chapter 6

• • • • • • • • • • • •

The Sugar Bowl was jammed with customers after the hockey game. Most of them were Flyers fans, and so they were quieter than they would have been after a win. At one booth, Francine, Binky, Arthur, Muffy, and the Brain were having milk shakes. Assorted coats, hats, and mittens were sandwiched in around them.

"Ooowwww!" said Binky, rubbing his elbow. "Has anyone ever figured out how hard ice really is?"

"There have been studies," said the Brain. "Tests have shown that compared to steel or —"

"Yeah, yeah," said Binky. "Just tell me they decided ice was hard."

The Brain nodded. "That was definitely confirmed."

"It's slippery, too," said Francine. "I was faked out four times on defense and fell. Poor Buster. We really left him on his own."

"Speaking of Buster," said Arthur, "where is he?"

"I thought he would be here," said the Brain. "I know I told him we were coming."

"He mumbled something about going home," said Binky. "He said he wasn't very hungry. I think he felt bad about losing the game for us."

"Binky," said Arthur. "Buster didn't lose the game."

"Well, he's the one who was scored on."

"Only because the rest of us didn't do our jobs."

"Maybe," said Binky. "But I don't think

Buster looked at it like that. He went off talking to himself again."

"I asked him about that," said Arthur. "He said I was imagining it. He said, 'If I start talking to myself, Arthur, you'll be the first to know.' "

"Hmmm," said the Brain. "But he has been doing that a lot lately."

"Even on the ice," said Francine. "Did you see him make those sudden lunges when the puck got close to him? It was almost like he didn't figure out what to do until the last second — and only after he discussed it with himself."

"How are we doing?" asked Coach Simard, passing by with his family. "I see some pretty long faces."

"We've been better," said Binky.

"Cheer up," said the coach. "Win or lose, early games are just samplers."

"What do you mean?" asked Francine.

"There's a lot going on right now. You're

finding out about your own skills and how those skills mesh with everyone else's. These things take time. The true test comes afterward."

Binky gulped. "There's a test?" he gasped.

"Relax, Binky. Not that kind. The test is simply what we learn from all the samplers. As we go along, we'll see which pieces fit best, and which we need to replace." He smiled. "So just relax, and I'll see you at the next practice." He continued toward the door.

"Did you hear that?" said Muffy. "The coach said we made a good start."

Binky shook his head. "He has to say that. Coaches always try to cheer up their players after they lose."

"Well, it still helps," said Arthur. "I just wish Buster could have heard it."

"Don't worry about Buster," said the Brain. "He's tough. He bounces back like a bungee cord. I'm sure he's doing just fine."

Chapter 7

• • • • • • • • • • • •

"Buster!"

Mrs. Baxter was standing in the doorway outside his bedroom.

"I'm not here," said a voice under the blanket.

"Come on, Buster. Cheer up."

"Not possible," said the voice.

His mother sighed. "It's not the end of the world."

Buster poked his head out. "Close enough. Did you see that headline?"

"Of course, I saw it. SLIPPERY START FOR FLYERS. I didn't write it, but I've certainly seen worse."

"Well, I'll bet you haven't seen worse articles where your son was mentioned by name. Did you catch the part about my tentative play?"

"But, Buster, it's only the first game. Look on the bright side. When you get better, there will be that many more good things to write about."

"HA!" Buster rolled over and stared at the ceiling. He tried to imagine some way that his life could get worse. There was the possibility of a meteor falling on him. Or an earthquake could swallow him up.

No, Buster thought. Those would only be improvements since they would get him out of his present condition.

"Why are you lying there like that?"

Buster groaned. "The game."

"Do not remind me. I almost had to cover my eyes. But you cannot give up."

"Why not?"

The ghost snorted. *"Do you think it was always so easy for me?"*

Jacques's ghost was standing next to the bed. He was still dressed in his full uniform — in fact, Buster had never seen him dressed any other way. It was as if he always wanted to be ready in case he was suddenly called back on the ice.

"You must try harder," said Jacques. *"True, you have eaten the peanut butter and tuna fish, but have you tasted horseradish pancakes? Make no mistake, that will put the fire in your belly."*

"Buster!" his mother called out. "Arthur's here."

Buster sat up as Arthur walked in.

"Hi, Buster. I came to see how you were doing."

"Terrible. Have you seen the paper?"

Arthur nodded. "But 'tentative' isn't such a bad word. It just means you're cautious.

Careful. That's a good thing. Besides, Buster, this isn't only about you."

"What do you mean?"

"It's the Flyers who lost, not Buster Baxter by himself. How do you think the rest of us feel?"

"I don't know. But I'm the one who let in the goals."

Arthur sighed. "That just means you were the last one to make a mistake, not the only one."

Buster had not thought about it like that. "I guess that's true," he said. "But it doesn't really change things. I wanted to leap and dart like the great Jacques Nettoyer. Instead I lunged and fell like the ordinary Buster Baxter."

Arthur bit his lip.

"What?" said Buster.

"Nothing."

"Come on, Arthur. . . . Tell me."

"Well, I was just thinking that if you're

having so much trouble imitating Jacques, maybe you should try something different."

"*Do not listen to him*," said the ghost. "*What does he know about hockey?*"

"No matter how many peanut butter and tuna sandwiches you eat," Arthur went on, "you're still always going to be Buster. So maybe genuine Buster is better than imitation Jacques."

"*He talks nonsense. Why are you even listening?*"

For once Buster ignored Jacques. "You know, Arthur," he admitted, "I like the sound of that."

Chapter 8

• • • • • • • • • • •

"I'm not fast enough," said Buster. "That's the problem."

He was talking to Coach Simard at one end of the hockey rink. The coach had agreed to meet with Buster for a little extra practice.

The coach tapped his stick on the ice.

"I think you're looking at this all wrong," he said. "You can only be so fast, Buster. But that isn't a problem, it's just a fact. What you do with that fact is the important thing."

"But Jacques Nettoyer was the greatest goalie ever — and he was fast."

"True. But was Jacques Nettoyer the only great goalie in league history?"

Buster thought about this. "I guess not."

"Okay, then. And were all these goalies fast? Did they play exactly the same way?"

"No," Buster admitted. "Stonewall Mason was known for his toughness. And Rick 'The Kick' Roquette was known for his fancy foot-saves."

"So if there's more than one way to be a great goalie, maybe you've just picked the wrong one to model yourself on."

"Do not listen to this silly man," said Jacques, appearing suddenly beside Buster. *"His head is full of pudding."*

Buster hesitated. "So what can I do?" he asked the coach.

"You have to find the approach that works for you, the one and only Buster Baxter."

"Do you think there is such a thing?"

Coach Simard laughed. "Of course. But finding out what that approach is may not be easy."

Buster took his position in front of the net while the coach skated back and forth, shooting pucks from different angles.

"Try this. . . . And this. . . ."

Each time the coach fired the puck, Buster tried to make a save.

"*Up . . . down . . .*," said Jacques. "*Oh, you missed another. You are driving me crazy!*"

"Sorry," said Buster.

"There's nothing to be sorry about," said Coach Simard, skating up to him. "We're just trying to find your strengths. Let's think. . . . If you're not comfortable trying to beat the puck to the goal, then you have only one choice."

"What's that?"

"You already have to be in the right place ahead of time."

Buster looked puzzled. "How can I do that? I can't read the puck's mind."

"In a way, you can. It's called anticipation."

"Anticipation?"

"That's right, Buster," said the coach. "When a player lines up to take a shot, the angle of his body and his stick give off clues to where the puck will go. Oh, sure, the player can fake one way and dart another, but even so, at the last moment, you still get a split second of advance warning."

"This is not my approach. Pay no attention. We will try again later."

But Buster looked encouraged. "It can't be easy," he said.

"That's true," the coach admitted. "Learning to read those signs takes time. But eventually you can get to the right spot ahead of the puck. And if you're already in the right place, being fast doesn't matter so much."

Buster thought this over. "It sounds good to me." He looked around to see what Jacques would say now.

But Jacques was gone.

Chapter 9

· · · · · · · · · · · ·

Buster was lacing up his skates behind the bench when a pair of thick legs appeared in front of him.

"Hi, Binky," he said without looking up.

Binky set his jaw. "Ready for the game?"

"I guess so."

"You *guess so?*" Binky crossed his arms. "Guessing isn't good enough, Buster. Now I know the first game was a little rough. . . . "

"What Binky is trying to say," added the Brain, coming up with Francine and Arthur, "is that you're not all by yourself out there on the ice."

"We'll be out there, too," said Francine. "And we'll try to make up for last time."

"I thought that was my fault," said Buster. "I let you down."

"Oh, no," said Arthur. "There was plenty of blame to go around."

"We felt bad leaving you in the shooting gallery," said the Brain.

"It won't happen again," Francine insisted.

As the first period started, Buster felt a little lonely in the net. Even if he wasn't following Jacques's advice, he still missed his company.

"All right, Buster, heads up," said the Brain, skating by.

"We'll cover you," said Binky from the side.

"Stay alert," said Arthur.

Buster smiled. Maybe he wasn't so alone, after all.

The Flyers' opponents, the Icehawks, were known for their explosive speed and for dumping the puck aggressively into the far end whenever possible. As they made their first run down the ice, Buster watched them closely.

The forward wants to fake me out, thought Buster, *but from that angle, he really only has my upper-left corner to shoot at.*

Buster shifted to his left and raised his arm.

The next moment the Icehawk player fired a slap shot that hit Buster's extended glove just as he opened it.

Glove save!

"Nice going, Buster!" said Arthur. "I thought he had you."

Buster breathed a sigh of relief and settled down to work. The Icehawks were not going to give up easily. They came at him from every angle. Again and again, Buster tried to figure out what would happen be-

fore it happened and position himself in advance. After his fourth save, Coach Simard gave him a big thumbs-up from the bench.

"It is a close game, is it not?" said a familiar voice to the side.

Buster smiled. He got a warm feeling inside knowing that Jacques had returned.

"They are a strong team, but I think you may have the advantage. Their goalie is nothing more than a block of ice. He will be shattered soon enough."

Buster watched as the two centers faced off at the opposite end. "And what about our goalie?" he asked.

"You are managing well enough."

"Does that mean you were wrong before?"

Jacques snorted. *"I am never wrong."* He paused. *"But it is possible that I was a little hasty in forming a judgment. This new style does seem to suit your game. You will never be* a cat, but you cannot deny your nature. And since you have learned that, it is time for me to go."

"Can't you stay? It's only the first period."

"There are other games and other players, my friend. I go where I am needed, and I am needed here no more. Au revoir. Good-bye, Buster."

"Well, thank you," said Buster, and he watched Jacques fade as he skated away.

Chapter 10

• • • • • • • • • • • •

BZZZZZZZZZZ

The final buzzer sounded, and Buster banged his stick on the ice in triumph. The Flyers had led the whole way, winning 4–1. The only goal against Buster had come on a power play, and even then he knew that he couldn't always anticipate everything.

"Way to go, Buster!"

"You really shut them down."

Buster saw his mother standing by the boards, and he skated over to see her.

"That was a nice game, honey," she said. "You really put the pedal to the metal."

"Mom, there are no cars in hockey." Buster craned his neck around her. He seemed to be looking for something.

"Where's Jimmy?" he asked.

Mrs. Baxter sighed. "There was a fire down at the old corn-canning factory. The intense heat created a blizzard of popped corn. There's never been anything like it before. Everyone's been pulled off other stories to get down there."

Buster frowned. His first moment of goalie glory, and no one was around to record it.

"Everyone but me, that is," his mother added.

"Are you going to write the story?" Buster asked.

His mother nodded.

"Does that mean I'll get my name in the headline?"

Mrs. Baxter thought for a moment. "You may have a ghost of a chance," she said.

Buster laughed. "That's good enough for me," he said, and went off to celebrate with his friends.

How to Pronounce the French in This Book

Page 1

Jacques Nettoyer \zhahk nuh' twah yā\

Page 18

Bonjour, mes amis \bōn zhur' māz ah mē'\
Hello, my friends

Oui \wē\ Yes

Page 19

Ah, non, Monsieur Binky
\ah nō muh syuh' bēn' kē\ Ah, no, Mr.
Binky

Page 21

Mais non \mā nō\ But no

C'est vrai \sā vrā\ That's true

Page 50

Au revoir \ō re vwah\ Good-bye